ORCA
YOUNG
READERS

Five Stars
for Emily

Kathleen Cook Waldron

ORCA BOOK PUBLISHERS

National Library of Canada Cataloguing in Publication Data
Waldron, Kathleen Cook
Five starts for Emily / Kathleen Cook Waldron.

(Orca young readers)
ISBN 1-55143-296-X

I. Title. II. Series.

PS8595.A549F59 2004   jC813'.54   C2004-901650-4

Library of Congress Control Number: 2004103570

Summary: When Emily's Aunt Hannah takes her to a northern cabin without electricity in the dead of winter instead of to Disneyland, Emily is furious.

Free teachers' guide available.

Orca Book Publishers gratefully acknowledges the support for its publishing programs provided by the following agencies: the Government of Canada through the Book Publishing Industry Development Program (BPIDP), the Canada Council for the Arts, and the British Columbia Arts Council.

Cover design by Lynn O'Rourke
Cover & interior illustrations by Hanne Lore Koehler

In Canada:
ORCA BOOK PUBLISHERS
BOX 5626, STN.B
VICTORIA, BC CANADA
V8R 6S4

In the United States:
ORCA BOOK PUBLISHERS
PO BOX 468
CUSTER, WA USA
98240-0468

07 06 05 04 • 6 5 4 3 2 1

Printed and bound in Canada
Printed on 100% post-consumer recycled paper,
100% old growth forest free, processed chlorine free
using vegetable, low VOC inks.

For my mother and family,
who remember Aunt Jerri, Aunt Hannah
and our adventures together.

Also for you, kind readers.
I hope you will enjoy your time
with Emily as much as I have.
—K.C.W.

Growing up isn't all it's cracked up to be.

I'm ten-and-a-half years old, and as far as I can tell, growing up means I have to dress myself, tie my own shoelaces, set the table, wash the dishes and make lunches for my little brother Jake and me. The list grows longer all the time. My reward for all these chores is that I get to stay up half an hour later than Jake does.

I don't mind the extra chores. I don't even mind having to read my own bedtime stories, but I don't like giving up my comforts.

When I was four, Mom made my favorite blanket into a T-shirt for me. She told me

1

this way I could wear my blanket instead of having to carry it. That seemed like a good idea until it fell apart. Now Mom uses it for a rag, and I have to pretend I'm too grown up to care.

I know that's baby stuff, and I'm pretty much over it, but the last time my ex-friend Jesse spent the night, she laughed at my Popeye night-light. She made me unplug it, and I had to wait till she was asleep before I could plug it in again and go to sleep myself.

The next morning she told me she was tired of always having to spend the night at my house. I'd have to stay all night at her house before she'd come back to mine. I guess that was her way of reminding me that the last two times I tried to sleep over at her place, her dad had to bring me home in the middle of the night. It wasn't my fault that I couldn't sleep in her bed. She was mean to blame me for something I couldn't help, and that's why Jesse is now my ex-friend.

Jake says I'm a fraidy-cat, but I'm not. I

just have a wild imagination. That's what Mom says.

I don't go to scary movies like other kids at school because the scary pictures stick in my imagination and I have nightmares for weeks. I don't play most video games for the same reason. I don't even play sports because when I see other kids running too close to me, I imagine my bones getting smashed and mashed and blood pouring all over me.

I like non-scary fun, like shopping at a mall where everything is marked down to half price or less. My biggest dream is to go to Disneyland because it has fun, safe rides *and* shopping.

I may never find the mall of my dreams, but I am going to Disneyland. In December, Aunt Hannah is taking me for what she calls our "five-star holiday." She doesn't have any kids of her own, so when her nieces and nephews turn ten, she takes us for a five-star holiday. This year it's my turn! I'm ten-and-a-half and ready to go. I only have one more month to wait.

Aunt Hannah hasn't told me where we're going yet; she likes to keep it a surprise until the last minute. But I'm sure we're going to Disneyland. Every time I've talked to her this year, I've hinted about it. I know she'd love it. She likes carnival rides and fireworks, and she loves shopping. She even has a job in shopping or marketing or something like that.

Not only that, but I heard her say she's ready for a different holiday this year.

Three years ago she took my oldest cousin, Tamara, to Mexico for *her* five-star holiday. Tamara told me she soaked in sunlight on the beach every day and tasted fresh coconut milk right out of the shell. She even spent two nights with a Mexican girl she met and learned a little Spanish. *Adiós amigo.*

Last year my next oldest cousin, Justin, went to Hawaii for *his* five-star holiday. He built sandcastles on the beach and ate pineapples and papayas until his belly bulged. He snorkeled face to face with parrotfish and sea turtles. At night he watched videos in a fancy hotel room while Aunt Hannah went dancing with her friends.

That nature stuff was perfect for Justin and Tamara. They love swimming and beaches, but I think Aunt Hannah has sipped enough coconut milk.

Five-star holiday! Mickey Mouse! Small World! Shopping spree! Here I come!

2

"This year," Aunt Hannah says, "for our five-star holiday, we're going to do something different."

A smile spreads across my face.

Aunt Hannah smiles back. "This year, Emily, we're going north instead of south!"

"North?" I say. The word freezes in my throat; my own breath chokes me. "Why would anyone go *north* in the *winter*?"

Aunt Hannah is still smiling. "It will be fun," she says.

"But *why*?" I ask.

"We're invited to a party!" she says. "A housewarming party!"

"What other kind of party would you have up north in the winter?" I ask.

Aunt Hannah ignores my question. "The party will be Saturday night," she tells me, "but we'll arrive a couple of days early so we can help set up. I haven't seen Dale or Becky in years. Now you and I will have our five-star holiday, and I'll get to see my old friends again. It's just too perfect."

"How long has it been since you've seen these people?" I ask, swallowing hard.

"We were school friends years ago, but we lost touch. I'm always busy, and they're always moving. Until now, I never knew where they were, only where they'd been. I'll bet they've moved a dozen times in the last ten years."

"Aunt Hannah," I say, trying to sound reasonable, "Canadians don't go north in the winter. It's...it's un-Canadian. Besides, what would we do there?"

"People will be coming for the whole weekend with skis, skates, snowshoes—all kinds of winter sports gear. We'll play all day and eat and dance all night. We'll stay a few days after the party as well, to soak in some peace and quiet."

Eating is the only item on that list that interests me, and I can do that at home. "Aunt Hannah, you can dance anywhere, and if it's winter sports you want, you can drive to Whistler or Grouse Mountain any winter day and find snow all over the place. Why spend our five-star holiday in the snow?"

"It will be fun," Aunt Hannah repeats, showing me a homemade invitation. The picture glued to the front shows a squatty log house surrounded by shadowy evergreens and mountains. And piles and piles of snow.

"Aunt Hannah," I say, taking a deep breath, "this looks more like a scene from Siberia than a party invitation."

"Emily, listen to me."

I stare at the madwoman who has taken over my aunt's body while my holiday stars quietly disappear.

"Last spring," she explains, "Dale and Becky moved up north, near Canoe Lake.

(*Blink, there goes the first star.*) They started building a log cabin in the mountains. (*Blink, another star vanishes.*) Their cabin isn't quite finished, (*Blink*) but they're having a housewarming anyway. (*Blink*) Isn't that wonderful?" (*Blink*)

My stars are gone. Gone with Mickey Mouse and the warm California sun. What can I do? I have to think fast.

"There's nothing I'd like more than a holiday with you, Aunt Hannah," I say, "but maybe I should wait till next year, when you're ready to warm up again. I could let Jake take my turn this year." I suggest this even though my younger brother is only eight. "He plays hockey, and he's always wanting more ice time. A winter holiday up north would be perfect for him."

"Emily!"

There is no talking her out of it. It's north or nowhere. Before I can say another word, Aunt Hannah adds more.

"And guess what, Emily," she says, flashing her biggest smile. "Dale and Becky have a daughter, Blossom, who's *just your age*!"

NO! The last time Aunt Hannah found someone *just my age*, it was a boy three years older, five inches taller and forty pounds heavier who spent an entire afternoon practicing karate on me. Now it's a girl, *just my age*. This isn't a holiday Aunt Hannah's planning. It's a disaster!

3

Arctic expeditions have packed less gear. Aunt Hannah packs food, sleeping bags, long underwear, skates, skis, snowshoes, a toboggan, her fiddle. The list goes on. My shorts sit sadly in the drawer while I pack sweaters and socks.

With all my hopes and dreams crushed to snow cones, I try to look on the bright side. "I'll take the money I've saved from my allowance," I say, tucking my Game Boy into the pocket of the jacket I'll be wearing in the car. "I might find some good bargains up there."

Jake laughs. "Why take anything?" he says. "We all know Aunt Hannah will have

to bring crybaby Emily back home before she even sees the highway."

Ignoring his stupid remark, I tell Mom, "Canoe Lake probably has lots of different shops. Don't you think, Mom?"

"You never know," Mom says, tossing an extra pair of thick socks into my duffel bag.

The night before we leave, I lie in bed wide-awake. My eyes won't close, so I walk to the window, pull the curtains apart and look for a star to wish on. It's raining, so I'll have to wish on a streetlight instead.

I know star and birthday wishes can come true, even if sometimes they get a little twisted. Before Jake was born, I wished for a big sister, and I got him instead. I wished for a piano, and I got a ukulele. I wished to be the most popular girl in school and ended up getting dumped by my best and only friend, Jesse. Now I don't have any friends at all. Maybe I'll skip wishing tonight and just hope really hard that in the morning Aunt Hannah will show me two tickets to Disneyland and tell me that going north was just a joke.

Aunt Hannah is ready to leave before sunrise. Mom and Dad get up to see me off, but Jake won't leave his warm bed. "Why should I get up to say goodbye?" he says. "We all know the wimp will be home before supper."

"Goodbye, Jake," I tell him. My manners are a lot better than his.

Aunt Hannah and I splash through the dark rain, climb into her cold car and begin our no-star holiday. I wave to Mom and Dad until the car turns a corner. Aunt Hannah turns on the radio, finds a song she likes and starts singing along. I pull out my Game Boy. Aunt Hannah is in high spirits. When we hit the highway, she switches off the radio and shouts, "We're going to a party in the mountains, and I'm taking my fiddle."

"Come on, Emily," she coaxes. "We're going to a party in the mountains, and I'm taking my fiddle..."

"Okay," I say. "We're going to a party in the mountains, and I'm taking a fiddle and my crazy Aunt Hannah."

Before long we've named everything in the car, from apples to underwear, that we're taking to our party in the mountains. We pass Abbotsford and Chilliwack. Houses get farther and farther apart. Trees crowd the side of the road. Mountains look steeper, shadows darker. The rain falls harder. I try to keep my mind on my Game Boy.

"Soon we'll be beyond Hope," Aunt Hannah says. She finds this funny.

My eyelids droop. Maybe I'll be like Rip van Winkle and sleep through my winter holiday. If I'm lucky, I'll wake up to summer. Who knows? Maybe, if I sleep long enough, I'll wake up to palm trees in my own backyard. We studied global warming at school. It *could* happen.

Suddenly the world disappears. We've been swallowed by a tunnel. Seconds later, just as suddenly, we're spit out again.

"That's just the first tunnel," Aunt Hannah assures me. "Two or three more and we'll hit my favorite: Hell's Gate." Aunt Hannah pulls a strand of her scouring pad hair and lets it spring back. When she was a baby, people probably liked her tight curls; now she could scrub pots with them.

Holey mountains keep leaping up in front of us.

"Here come the Gates of Hell," Aunt Hannah announces cheerfully, "and in we go."

Hell's Gate is no different from the other tunnels, except it has no lights, and it has another, longer, tunnel right after it. I play with my Game Boy until I can barely lift my eyelids. I hear our wheels turning on the pavement. Rain slashes the car. More tunnels ambush us. The rain turns to sleet. Cliffs lurch up from nowhere with spikes of frozen waterfalls clinging to their sides.

"Pull my tree book out of the pile there, Emily," Aunt Hannah says, "and tell me what kind of trees these are."

I find her tree book and open it.

"Are they pine or spruce or fir?" Aunt Hannah asks.

"Furry trees?" I ask.

"That's f-i-r, Emily, not f-u-r."

"Oh," I say. "Too bad. I like the idea of fuzzy trees."

"Look at the bark, Emily. Does it look wavy like cardboard or flaky like cornflakes? Do the needles look long and soft or short and stiff?"

Dark bark. Green branches. Beats me. "I think they're spruce trees," I tell her, though I haven't a clue. Not one of these trees looks anything like the trees in our backyard.

"Spruce," she repeats with a smile. "Good, that settles it."

Out my window, ice, snow, trees and rocks leap up beside us and vanish. Snow, like Uncle Bill's dandruff, begins to fall in fat flakes. The world grows smaller and smaller. Maybe we'll be lost in a blizzard. Frozen till spring. Or buried in an avalanche, stiff as icicles, for thousands of years. It *could* happen.

"I can't see a darn thing," Aunt Hannah mutters, squinting through the windshield. "We may as well stop for gas."

We pull off the road to fill the tank and empty our bladders. The moment I open the car door, I'm attacked by a blast of cold. I have to wade through a sea of slush to go inside.

I've never had to use a gas station washroom before. I don't see it anywhere. I'll have to ask a stranger where it is, and then a total stranger will know my private business.

"Excuse me," I say to the bubble-blowing gum chewer behind the counter, "where's the washroom?"

"There's the key," she replies between bubbles, pointing to a small key dangling from a hunk of metal, big and heavy enough to be a weapon. *Ladies* is painted on it with pink nail polish. If this is the ladies' key, what does the men's key look like?

Bubbles points to the door. "Go back outside (*chew, chew*) and around the right side of the building (*chew*). You can't miss it." (*Blow—Pop!*)

I step back into the cold. If I stay close to the side of the building, maybe I'll avoid at least some of the wind and slush. I fit the key into the door marked with a stick figure in a skirt. From past experience at malls, I know I don't actually have to be wearing a skirt to go inside.

"Em," Aunt Hannah says, stepping up behind me and placing her hand over mine on the key, "I can't wait a moment longer. Let me run in first. I'll just be a second."

She pushes the door open and squeezes inside, leaving me out in the cold. I lean against the wall. She'll just be a second, I keep reminding myself. I may as well wait here.

By the time Aunt Hannah opens the door again, my toes are numb and I wonder if my feet have frozen to the ground. "Thanks, dear," she says, handing me the key and pushing past me.

Inside the washroom, the light flickers and buzzes. The floor is covered with scraps of paper. I move as quickly as I can, touching as little as possible.

When I return the key, Aunt Hannah is at the counter paying for the gas. While she and Bubbles chat, I study the different gas station snacks.

Walking back to our car, Aunt Hannah asks, "Are you hungry?"

My stomach growls "empty" before my voice can answer.

She pulls a basket out of the backseat and says, "Restaurant food can be terribly overpriced and greasy. So I made us a nice healthy picnic."

A picnic? In a blizzard? As far as I can remember, my picnics were always in the summer, in a park, with green grass. Never in a parking lot with snow.

Aunt Hannah hands me a sandwich. I take a bite. It scorches my mouth like wildfire. I choke.

"It's Cajun-style tofu," Aunt Hannah explains with a smile. "I made it myself."

"I may have gotten it a bit too spicy," she admits while I continue to choke, "but, you know, red pepper is really very soothing once it reaches your stomach."

I gulp the warm celery juice she pours from her thermos. Restaurant food may be greasy and overpriced, but I'll take it any day over this.

We eat in silence, our breath and the celery juice steaming up the windows. Snow continues to fall. I try to follow a single snowflake as it spins in the wind. By the time we finish eating, the storm has let up enough for Aunt Hannah to see.

We set off slowly in our rolling snow bubble. "Let's play the alphabet game," Aunt Hannah suggests. "*A* is for aspens by the road."

My turn. "*B* is for boulders, bare and cold."

C, D, E, F, G.

My turn. "*H* for house. Mine's far away."

Aunt Hannah. "*I* for ice, all over the place." Wonder how she thought of that.

Ice, snow, trees, rocks. Ice, snow, trees, rocks. I play Game Boy until the screen fades to black. Drat, the batteries are dead. Game Boy is gone, just like the stars in my holiday. I must have twenty extra pairs of socks, but not a single extra battery. I tuck my Game Boy into my pocket and go back to trying to pick out snowflakes.

By the time we stop for dinner, the snow has stopped and we're on *X* of our second alphabet game. "*X!* Moose crossing!" Aunt Hannah shouts. "See the *X* on the sign?"

"*Y!*" I reply. "*Y* are we doing this?"

"Not fair," Aunt Hannah replies. "*Why* doesn't start with a *Y*."

"I'm looking, Aunt Hannah, believe me," I say, searching for something, anything, in this wilderness that starts with *Y*.

For dinner I actually get to eat a greasy, overpriced restaurant meal. Aunt Hannah orders a bowl of lentil soup and a pot of herbal tea. But I have a burger, fries and a hot fudge sundae. It may be the last chance I have to eat anything normal.

"I was just thinking, Emily," Aunt Hannah says cheerfully, between sips of tea. "This must be the farthest away from home you've ever been. Even that silly camp you left early was closer than this."

The hot fudge that tasted so creamy only a moment ago suddenly tastes like paste. "Thanks for reminding me, Aunt Hannah." I lay my spoon on my plate. Dinner is finished.

Last summer the counselors at that stupid sleepover camp put me on the bus alone, just because I wanted to go home more than I wanted to sleep in a creepy little cabin with a bunch of mean girls.

Back in the car, it's so dark I see only shadows of ice, snow, trees and rocks. My head droops. My neck jerks it back up. Droop, jerk, droop, jerk...Even in my dreams, snow, ice, trees and rocks keep sliding by.

A hand on my shoulder makes everything stop.

"Wake up, Emily," Aunt Hannah says. "We're here."

4

I rub my eyes and look outside. Snow! Snow everywhere. I open the car door and step outside. Cold slices through my clothes and the thin soles of my boots. A log cabin cowers in the snow.

Pale yellow light escapes from its windows and falls on the snow. We slam the car doors and start walking. A sharp *rrowff* shatters the silence. A black shadow charges toward us.

"BEAR! Run!" I scream, trying to push Aunt Hannah back to the car. "Hurry. Let's get out of here!" The cabin door flies open. A tall man with wild hair and a shaggy beard grins in the doorway. "Hurry, Aunt Hannah! Run!" I shout.

And Aunt Hannah does run. Right to the house. Right to the man. She runs with the bear that is now wagging its tail and licking the man's hand. Aunt Hannah and the hairy man throw their arms around each other.

"Dale, this is my niece, Emily," Aunt Hannah says, turning toward me.

Dale smiles a big hairy smile. "And this is Murphy, our Newfie," he says, scratching the ears of what I now see is a big black dog. Dale pulls on a huge jacket. "I'll bring in your stuff," he says. "You go inside. Becky's putting on the kettle."

Inside the cabin, the light is dim and the walls are bumpy—logs. The walls in the entryway are lined with wooden shelves heaped with hats, mitts and scarves. Jackets and skates hang from wooden pegs. Off to one side is a big wooden box, filled with wood. I've never seen so much wood in one place.

A tall woman greets us, wiping her hands on a bright green apron. She and Aunt Hannah hug like it's the end of the world—Becky.

29

Aunt Hannah takes off her boots. As I bend down to pull mine off, a voice behind me says, "You must be Emily." I turn around.

"Blossom?" I say to a girl who has more freckles than a beach has sand.

"I didn't think you'd ever get here," Blossom says.

"Neither did I" is all I can think of to say.

For a moment we stand in silence. How long can a week be? I wonder.

"Leave your coat in the mudroom and come inside," Blossom says. "It's freezing out here."

She's got that right.

From the mudroom, we step into a big room that seems to be both kitchen and living room. Beyond the kitchen, a couch and chairs crowd around a wood heater, and a piano fills up a corner. Flickering candles and oil lamps cast shadows everywhere. It's hard to tell what's shadow and what's real. It's warm, though, and a fire crackles in the stove.

Blossom sits down at the kitchen table. I do the same. I expect Blossom to ask me about our drive or something, but she doesn't say a word. Maybe she's waiting for me to ask her something, but I can't think of anything. What do you say to a total stranger in a strange place?

"What kind of hockey skates do you have?" Blossom says at last.

"I don't have hockey skates." I knew Jake should have come instead of me. If only Aunt Hannah had listened.

"You didn't bring your skates?"

"I think Aunt Hannah packed an extra pair of figure skates that are my size."

"*Figure skates*?"

"Skates are skates, aren't they?"

"You don't play hockey?"

"No, but if it makes you feel any better, I don't figure skate either."

Blossom stares like I just dropped from outer space.

Becky interrupts our silence by handing us each a huge cup of steaming hot chocolate with marshmallows on top.

"Be careful," Becky warns, "it's hot."

No fresh coconut milk in the shell, but then I don't think cousin Tamara's coconut milk came with chocolate and marshmallows. Tamara never mentioned homemade chocolate chip cookies either, especially ones with more chocolate chips than cookie. I grab a handful.

"Save some for the rest of us, Emily," Aunt Hannah says.

I hope Blossom thinks the color rising in my face is from the steam in my cup. I hunch down over my cup and suck in a mouthful of melted marshmallow.

Dale brings in the last of our stuff. Murphy follows him inside, his toenails clicking on the wooden floor. While Dale pulls up a chair, Murphy finds a warm spot by the fire, paces off a small circle, curls up and drops his head on his paws with a loud *mmmmph.*

"Work has been one crisis after another," Aunt Hannah says with a sigh. "For the past few weeks, all that's kept me going has been thinking about you and all this lovely peace and quiet."

Dale, Becky and Aunt Hannah all start talking at once. Peace and quiet? Blossom and I couldn't squeeze in a word over all that chatter if we wanted to. I keep my eyes on my chocolate.

I swallow my last sip and lick the rim of the cup. "Where's your bathroom?" I whisper to Blossom.

"Outside," she answers.

"Outside?"

"Outside," she repeats.

"You mean like at a gas station?"

"I mean outside, like *outside*."

5

"We plan to have an inside bathroom next summer. And electricity," Blossom adds.

"That's nice, but what I have to do won't wait till summer."

Blossom shrugs.

"It's dark out there," I say. "Where's the light?"

"There's a flashlight by the door."

"I don't know where to go." Panic grabs hold of me. Outside? Alone? In the dark? I want to go home.

"Take Emily to the outhouse, Blossom," Becky says, interrupting the grown-up chatter fest. "I'll get her some snow boots and a warmer jacket."

Blossom scrunches up her freckles, but she does as she's told. The boots and jacket feel big and bulky. Blossom flicks on a flashlight and we step outside.

Once again, the icy cold stings my face and steals my breath. Blossom leads the way with the flashlight. I follow her every step. She stops and I bump into her back, almost falling down.

"The door's over there," she says, pointing.

I don't move.

"There," Blossom repeats.

My toes curl inside my boots.

"I thought you had to go," she says.

"I do. Is there a light?"

"Here, take the flashlight, or there's a candle inside you can light."

"I'll take the flashlight."

Blossom starts to walk back to the house.

"Wait! Where are you going?"

"It's cold out here, and I thought you might like some privacy. Besides, it's not like you won't be able to find your way back. You can't miss the house."

"Wait, I'll be quick." I reach for the out-house door, but stop cold. What's inside? Spiders? Bats?

"Is it stuck?" Blossom asks, walking toward the door. "There's a little wooden latch on the frame that you have to turn. It keeps the wind from blowing the door off its hinges when no one is out here." She flips the latch, opens the door and steps aside.

Nothing jumps out. I point the flashlight inside. It isn't as creepy and cobwebby as I expected. It's clean, cleaner than the gas station washroom, but just as smelly. All I see is a hole and a coffee can. There's a picture on the wall, but it's too dark to tell what it is.

I close the door behind me and beam the flashlight at the hole. What's down there? Could I fall in and be trapped? Will something grab me when I sit down?

I step up to the hole and shine the flash-light down inside it. All I see is a pointy brown peak covered with white splotches.

YUCK! But Nature calls, and I can't wait any longer.

It doesn't take me long to figure out that toilet paper, not coffee, is in the can. Can't fool me. Quicker than I thought possible, I'm finished and out of there, ready to run back to the house.

"Wait," Blossom orders, taking the flashlight from me and stepping into the outhouse. "I may as well go too, while we're out here."

Darkness falls around me. Tears fill my eyes. This is it. I'll die out here. Freeze to death. Or be eaten by wild animals. I want to run, but I can't. Suddenly a loud, low *RRRRfffff* cuts through the night. I scream.

Blossom steps out of the outhouse, laughing. The door slams behind her and she latches it shut.

"What's so funny?" If she didn't have the flashlight, I'd flatten her.

"That's Murphy. Our dog, remember? He must have been asleep when we went out. Now he wants to come outside with us. What did you think he was? A bear?"

38

Back inside, we wash our hands and faces with warm water dipped from a pot on the stove into an enamel basin, and we brush our teeth with cold water pumped from a hand pump in the sink.

Blossom helps me carry my stuff upstairs to her room. We step through a doorway with no door, and she switches on a sort of flashlight-looking lamp. The outside wall is made of logs. I stare at the pink ceiling covered with plastic.

"That's insulation," Blossom explains. "Finishing the ceiling is another spring project."

"Why cover it up? It looks like cotton candy."

"Trust me, you don't want to touch it; it's really itchy," she tells me as I unroll my foamy on the floor and lay my sleeping bag on top.

"This isn't like any house I've ever seen."

Blossom flops down on her bed. "I know," she says. "I helped build it."

Then words rush from her mouth, like water bursting from a hose. She talks about hauling and peeling logs, notching

39

them and stacking them on top of each other, spiking them into place. Am I the first person she's told about all this?

"Are you telling me you can peel a log like a banana?"

"When spruce logs are green and sappy in the spring," she replies, "they're easy to peel. Fir logs are harder. You need a really sharp knife for them."

"Must be a pretty big knife, too," I say, reaching over and running my hand along one of the outside walls.

"You can use either a drawknife with two handles or a peeling spud."

"A peeling what?"

"Spud. It's like a sharp straightened-out hoe."

I haven't a clue what she's talking about. How can a knife have two handles? Isn't a *spud* a potato? "Your parents let you use knives like that?" I ask, trying to picture this freckle-faced girl attacking a log with a knife.

"They let me try," she admits, "but usually I just pulled the strips once they were started. You should have seen how black and sticky that pitch made my hands. Soap couldn't touch it."

"How did you clean your hands then?" I ask, but Blossom pays no attention. She's bombarding me again with words like "land clearing" and "slash burning." She might as well be describing life on Mars for all the sense it makes to me.

She only stops when Aunt Hannah, Dale and Becky come upstairs to say good-night. I try to catch Aunt Hannah's eye to let her know what a whacko she's leaving me with, but Aunt Hannah is oblivious. "Isn't this cozy?" she says, hugging me.

In spite of my now-crushed ribs, I answer, "Shouldn't we call Mom and Dad to let them know we're here?" I want to hear their voices. I want them to wish me goodnight. I want Jake to know I made it here—away from him. I want to go home.

"You mean phone them?" Aunt Hannah says, as if it's the strangest request she's ever heard. Everyone laughs but me.

Becky seems to be the only one who realizes that laughing at a guest is rude. "Sorry, dear," she explains, "but having no electricity means we also have no phone."

"That's okay. Aunt Hannah has a cell phone. Don't you, Aunt Hannah?"

"It won't work in these mountains, Emily. Your parents know that. They're not expecting a call."

"Goodnight, girls," Becky says.

"Don't stay up all night giggling," Dale warns. "We have a busy day tomorrow."

As soon as they turn off the light and head downstairs, Blossom starts talking again. I curl up in my sleeping bag, saying "yes," "no," "is that so" and "oh" about a million times. After that I just grunt. Blossom doesn't seem to notice.

Now she's talking about axes and chain saws. Is everything here sharp and dangerous? I could tell her about my new computer game and the funny video I just saw. There are plenty of interesting things I could tell her, if she'd ask.

Maybe she has some friends who aren't as weird as she is. There must be kids at school. Maybe she has some nice neighbors.

Blossom's voice drifts off into soft, even breathing. A shiver runs down my spine. Not a cold-outside shiver. No. This is worse. This is the first time since camp that I've been so far from home that I couldn't be back with Mom and Dad in five minutes. I can't even call them.

I listen to the wind and the muffled voices downstairs. The window is black. No streetlights give a hint of what's outside. No curtains keep whatever is out there from peeking in here. No cars drive by. No sirens. Only the wind tapping on the window. I lie still, breathing slowly.

Are Mom and Dad sleeping now? Jake must be asleep. Do they miss me? I miss them. What if they move away while I'm gone? I wouldn't even know where they were. I want my bed, my pillow, my Popeye night-light. Where's the Sandman when you need him?

C-R-A-C-K. A snap, loud and sharp, like a gunshot on TV.

"What was that?" I yell, just about jumping out of my sleeping bag. "Is someone shooting at us? Blossom? Aunt Hannah? Somebody, help!"

Blossom mumbles and rolls over. "Aunt Hannah!" I call louder.

I hear footsteps on the stairs. A burglar? A killer?

"It's okay, Emily," I hear Aunt Hannah say. "Hush now, or you'll wake up Blossom."

"Don't worry about Blossom," Becky says, following Aunt Hannah into the room. "She could sleep through anything."

"What happened? What was that noise?"

"It was just a log, checking," Becky says.

"Checking what?" I want to know.

"Cracking. House logs settle their first winter, and they tend to dry unevenly, especially when the temperature drops outside and we make the fire hotter inside."

"Will the logs break? Will the house fall down?"

Becky strokes my forehead. "No, dear, they're just as strong as ever."

"Will they crack all night?"

"No," Becky assures me, "it should be quiet from now on. You shouldn't have any trouble falling asleep."

How can I fall asleep in a crazy place like this, I want to ask, but they say goodnight and go back downstairs before I can say a word. Blossom is still sound asleep. Does she peel logs when she sleeps instead of sawing them? I don't hear her breathing now because music is drifting up the stairs, soft and soothing. How can they have a stereo without electricity?

I curl up in my sleeping bag. Music floats around me. A tear slides down my cheek. Maybe I should go downstairs and ask Aunt Hannah to take me home. Maybe we can still go some place where walls don't crack like gunshots, and the wind doesn't whistle and howl. Maybe.

6

My eyes open, then slam shut. I open them again, slowly. Where am I? Logs. Insulation. Blossom's room. The morning sunlight pouring through her window is so bright it hurts. At home the summer sunshine isn't this bright, much less the thin winter sun that seeps through the clouds.

Blossom's bed is empty. Breakfast smells float up the stairs. I crawl out of my sleeping bag, pull on my clothes and go down.

Everyone is seated around the kitchen table. All three adults are talking as if they never stopped to sleep. Blossom is spreading what looks like homemade jam on a steaming scone. A fire crackles in the heavy iron cookstove. Outside the snow sparkles. I mumble "good morning" and head for the bathroom. I remember the outhouse and decide to wait.

With warm water from a pitcher beside the kitchen sink, I wash my hands and face and brush my teeth while Becky piles a plate with bacon, eggs and potatoes. Normally I'd just load one or two of those hot scones with butter and jam, but this morning my stomach is rumbling, and the more food I give it, the happier it will be.

"After breakfast we'll clear off the skating rink," Blossom says. "It's our job to get it ready for the party."

"Okay," I say, without enthusiasm.

"First finish your math," Becky tells Blossom.

"You have homework during Christmas break?" I ask. "Gruesome."

"I have homework all the time. There's no school here so I do all my schoolwork at home."

I stare at her, not quite sure whether to say "Sweet" at the thought of never having to go to school or "Bummer" at the thought of endless homework.

So I say, "While you do your math, I'll just watch a video or some TV."

Everyone thinks this is funny.

"Sorry, Emily," Becky says, almost choking from laughing so hard. "It's just funny because we don't have a TV. You see, without electricity, television is a luxury."

Television a luxury. Is she kidding? Television is a fact of life, a necessity, like bathrooms and night-lights. I've never known anyone who didn't have a TV. They might not be on the Net, or they may only be allowed to watch certain shows at certain times, but everyone has a TV. "Didn't you have a television before you moved here?"

"Of course we did," Blossom says, a little too loudly.

"But we sold it," Becky adds, "to buy things that would be more useful here."

"Like drawknives and chain saws?" I say.

"Exactly," Becky says, impressed, no doubt, by my insight. "How did you know?"

49

"I have my ways," I say, "but it's too bad you don't have a TV. I bet you'd get great satellite reception out here."

"Oh, we do get that," Dale pipes in. "On a clear night we can go outside and count dozens of satellites as they go blinking by."

So much for television. A new idea strikes me. "What about shopping? I could check out the mall while Blossom finishes her homework."

More laughter. These people seem to think I'm a regular comedian.

"The only 'mall' you could check out here is the garbage dump," Becky tells me, wiping away tears of laughter with her apron.

No real mall? Not even a strip mall? "The garbage dump?" I repeat.

Becky explains, "If anyone has anything they no longer need that might still be useful to someone else, they set it aside at the dump. That way whoever needs it can just pick it up. It makes for great shopping opportunities. And the price is certainly right."

"Last summer we found a whole box of perfect canning jars without a single nick, chip or crack in the lot," Dale says.

"Before winter came, we had to be careful because there were almost always bears at the dump," Blossom adds with enthusiasm. "We had to wait in the truck until they decided to leave."

"Who needs a mall with all that?" I say.

"You're a fast learner, Emily," Dale says.

Aunt Hannah raises her eyebrow at me, but I ignore her. Where does she find friends like this? These people actually seem happy to be stuck in the middle of nowhere, watching satellites at night and spending their days shopping at the dump with bears.

While Blossom finishes her math, I go to the outhouse by myself. Murphy follows me. He can chase off any wild animals I might run into.

The outhouse isn't as scary in the daylight. It's just a little house with a hole in the middle. Again I check the hole, in case anything sleeping down there might have

51

woken up. Same brown peak with white paper splotches. Ugh!

To keep my mind off the hole, I sit and look at the outhouse picture. Three bears are sitting on a blanket with a big food basket. At the bottom is printed *Teddy Bears' Picnic*. The mama bear, wearing a straw hat and a red-checkered dress, is reaching into the picnic basket. I wonder what's inside.

Back at the house, Blossom is still writing numbers on paper.

Aunt Hannah is naming off chores. "You mean you have all this work to do before everyone arrives, and you haven't made a single list?" she says.

"Well, no. Not yet anyway." Becky sounds like me when I don't know the right answer at school.

"We can fix that right this minute," Aunt Hannah says, scooping a clean sheet of Blossom's paper and a pencil. "Let's see. We'll need a cooking list, a baking list, a shoveling list, a cleaning list."

Her pencil flies across the paper. No sooner does she write the word *firewood* than Dale offers me a lesson in hauling it and I accept.

By the time I've added a snowsuit, mitts and toque to all the other winter gear I have to wear, I'm not sure if I feel like Frosty the Snowman or a sausage. Murphy and I follow Dale outside. Dale shovels the path from the house to the woodshed while I pull a toboggan along behind us. Murphy runs back and forth between us.

"Not too much snow last night," Dale says as he scoops what looks to me like heaps of snow with the world's biggest shovel. "They say when it really snows around here you can watch fenceposts disappear. A car sitting outside will look like a mere bump under a soft white blanket. Imagine that."

"Awesome," I say, though I can't imagine it at all.

Dale shows me how to take down pieces of wood so the pile won't fall on me. How dumb does he think I am? There's a stack of wood and you take pieces off it. Next he shows me how to stack the wood on the toboggan.

"Got it, Dale," I tell him. "The wood is under control."

"Good," he says. "The woodbox is just inside the mudroom, and you can pull the toboggan right up to it. Thanks, Emily."

"No problem."

Murphy rolls around in the fresh snow while I pull pieces of wood off the pile and stack them on the toboggan. Six, seven, eight. The row I'm working on is getting a little lopsided, but I keep pulling down wood. Nine, ten, eleven. OOPS! A piece of wood comes loose, then another and another.

The pile collapses and wood crashes down everywhere. Murphy starts to bark, and I jump out of the way barely in time to keep from being crushed. The wood I stacked so carefully on the toboggan is scattered and buried. I could have been buried too, but no one seems to have noticed, except for Murphy.

"It's okay, boy," I tell him, patting his head and scratching behind his ears as

best I can with my thick mitts. He nuzzles his head under my arm.

I look around. Maybe someone will come and help me clean up this mess or tell me to forget the firewood and go back inside. I wait, but no one comes.

I sit down on a log. Murphy lies down beside me, sliding a log out of his way with his paws. I pull off my mitts and rub his tummy, surprised at how soft and warm it is. I've never had a dog; Mom says it isn't fair to keep a dog in the city. Murphy keeps my hands warm, but my feet are getting cold. I guess I'll have to fix this mess myself.

I pull the toboggan out from under the scattered pieces of wood and begin to load it again. When I'm dragging it back to the house, I have to stop several times to pick up the pieces that slip off. I slide the toboggan right inside and unload the wood into the woodbox. Silly me, I thought toboggans were for riding down hills for fun.

By the time Blossom finishes her homework, I've hauled three more loads. The woodshed is mostly cleaned up, and the woodbox is nearly full.

I'm ready for a nice long break, but Blossom is ready to go outside. "What size shoe do you wear?" she asks. "I think we have an extra pair of hockey skates that might fit you. You can't play hockey in figure skates, you know."

No, I don't know, but I don't say so. I watch her put on her winter gear. Then she reaches up on a shelf and pulls down a pair of scuffed brown skates. Next she hands me a hockey stick and a shovel. Stuffing a couple of pucks in her pocket, she slings her skates over her shoulder, grabs her own hockey stick and shovel, and walks out the door.

7

I follow Blossom down a narrow path with shoulder-high snow on both sides. We drag our shovels behind us, following a white path through a white world. I try to picture what's under the snow: fences, flowers, rocks, cars?

We pass Dale clearing another path with his big, flat snow scoop. Murphy runs up to us and licks Blossom's face.

"Where do all these paths go? Do you have barns or chicken coops or something?" I ask, as Murphy leaps through the snow beside us.

"The path Dad's shoveling goes to his toolshed. The one over there leads to the trailer where we store all our extra boxes of clothes and stuff."

"Do you have any animals besides Murphy? People in places like this have chickens and sheep and goats and cows, don't they?"

"I guess you do if you're a farmer or a rancher."

"You're not?"

"Not yet."

"What do your parents do then?"

"This is our first winter. We saved money for five years so we could move here, build our house and have some time to get used to things."

"Don't your parents have jobs? What do they do all day?"

"When they're not working on the house, Mom's been selling homemade peanut butter and granola, and Dad's been bucking firewood with a neighbor down the road."

"Bucking firewood?"

"Cutting firewood."

"Don't they have real jobs?"

"Those are real jobs. They work, and they get paid."

Murphy stops for a quick pat from Blossom, then lopes out in front of us. He looks like a black locomotive chugging through a white tunnel.

Looking back over my shoulder, I see Blossom's house perched on a hill. The trail isn't steep, but the ground falls steadily away from the house. Tall trees drop little snowstorms on us every time the slightest breeze blows. Murphy runs ahead and disappears.

"There *is* one animal here that I forgot to tell you about," Blossom announces. "His name is Blizzard Buster the Terrible. Snowflakes quake in their boots at the sight of him!" She straddles her snow shovel. Waving her hockey stick in the air, she gallops down the hill.

"Hi, ho, Blizzard Buster!" she shouts. Snow dumps down on her from the trees, turning her as white as the world around her, a snow ghost. I can still hear her voice, but she's so far in front of me that the snow soaks up her words. I follow her, keeping my eyes on the trail so I don't fall.

What are the other kids from school doing now? Are they at the mall with their friends, exchanging clunker Christmas presents for cool stuff on sale cheap? Are they meeting their mothers for lunch at the food court? Would they be ordering Chinese or a burger and fries? What would I order if I were at the food court now instead of out in the middle of nowhere?

THWACK! I walk right into Blossom, nearly knocking both of us down. This girl needs warning signals.

A big open area stretches out in front of us. We've reached the bottom of the hill. "Nice field," I say, trying to take in the wide, white flatness.

"It's not a field," Blossom explains. "It's a lake, Wolf Lake."

My jaws clamp shut, catching my tongue between my teeth. "Where are the wolves?" I spit out the words, mingled with salty blood from my tongue.

"There used to be wolves," Blossom says. "But no one has seen one for a long time. At least that's what the neighbors tell us."

I take a deep breath; air rushes over my tender tongue.

Blossom steps onto the frozen lake.

"How thick is the ice?" I ask, trying to sound casual.

"Dad said last time he checked it was thick enough to hold up an airplane."

Airplanes have wings. They can fly. I stay several steps behind Blossom. If she falls in, I want to be far enough back to stay dry, maybe even rescue her from icy death if I don't have to get wet.

After about fifty-three more steps, I see the outline of a rink that's been shoveled before. It's covered with fresh snow, drifted deep in some places, almost bare in others. At the side of the rink is a wooden plank laid across two stumps. At either end is a net, drifted over with snow. Blossom brushes the snow off the bench with her sleeve, drops her hockey stick, laces up her skates and starts pushing her shovel across the rink.

I sit down. "You look like you've done this before," I say.

"Not much to it," Blossom says. "It doesn't take a genius to find the smart end of a shovel, and you don't have to be a big-time wrestler to move a little snow. That's what my dad says. It's his idea of a joke."

"Do you ever do anything here besides work?"

"We can play hockey when the rink's clear," Blossom points out.

"I already told you, I don't skate."

"You don't skate. What do you do then?"

"I do all kinds of things."

"Like what?"

"Like shopping."

"I mean fun stuff."

"Shopping is fun."

"Okay then. What else?"

"I don't know, Game Boy, movies, TV."

"Don't you like sports?"

"Not especially."

"You must at least watch hockey on TV."

"Not if I can avoid it."

"What kind of Canadian avoids hockey? It's the greatest game in the world."

"The only thing I like about hockey is the Zamboni. If you had one, we could save a lot of time. Also, riding a big machine would be a lot more fun than pushing a stupid shovel."

As if to prove that a Zamboni has nothing on her, Blossom turns and starts shoveling faster. Fine with me. I close my eyes and try to pretend that the sound of her shovel scraping the ice is really the sound of a roller coaster climbing up its track. Any second now I'll fly down the other side, with the wind screaming against my face. But this roller coaster has only one speed—slow. I open my eyes. Blossom has cleared a narrow patch of ice. Behind her, snow devils spin around the lake.

I'd go home right now if I could. I'll bet my family misses me and wonders what I'm doing. Jake was sure I'd never make it this far. But I did. I've even spent the night. I can go home and tell him how totally wrong he was about me.

"Make way for the world's first and only human Zamboni," Blossom shouts. "This is the ice that skate blades dream of—smooth as glass and fast as light."

Murphy runs up to her, plowing snow with his nose. He crouches down and attacks the snow Blossom has just piled along the side of the rink. I have to laugh.

Blossom shovels harder. "The idea was that we'd both do this. That's why we brought two shovels."

"I know."

"This isn't a resort where all you do all day is lounge around."

"I've noticed."

"You're not doing me any favor by being here, you know. It wasn't my idea for you to come."

"I'm sure it wasn't."

"And guess what. I didn't ask to come here either."

"What?"

Still shoveling, Blossom says, "My parents move all the time. They say they like the adventure. We stay in one place just long enough for me to start making friends, then *whap*, we move again."

"Maybe after this you'll get to move somewhere better, like California."

"We've already done that."

"You have? You've been to Disneyland?"

"Yep."

"And you moved from there to come here?"

"That was about two moves ago. Or was it three? I lose track."

"How many times have you been to Disneyland?"

"Lots."

"How many is lots?"

"Too many. Whenever anyone came to visit, that's where we went. It's no big deal."

"It's a huge deal. How can you say that?"

"Maybe it's a big deal for you, but not for me. All I wanted to do was go to an NHL game, but I never went to a single one."

"Why not?"

"My parents don't approve of professional sports. They refuse to support overpaid athletes. They don't understand what a thrill it is to watch great hockey. They don't believe me when I tell them one day I'm going to play in the NHL."

"You?"

"I'm going to be a star. The first girl to play forward in the NHL. I'll be the best anyone ever saw. Now, come on," Blossom says, "lace up your skates and let's see just how bad a hockey player you are."

I look down at my boots and then out at the lake. The wind bites into my back.

"Are you waiting for the snow to melt?" she asks. "That should be in about four months."

"Okay, okay," I say, slipping my feet into the stiff, cold skates. "They're too big," I announce, feeling relieved.

"I thought they might be," Blossom says. She pulls an extra pair of socks out of her snowsuit pocket. "That's why I brought these."

She tosses the socks to me and speeds off across the ice, guiding the puck with her stick. That looks easy enough, I tell myself. Maybe I *could* do it. I tie double knots in my skate laces, reach for my stick and stand up.

Phoomf! My feet fly out from under me. Blossom skates over and gives me a hand up. *Ooomf!* I fall again. Murphy comes over and licks my face.

"Is this your first time on skates?" Blossom asks, telling Murphy to go lie down. He finds a soft spot in the snow and makes himself comfortable. He's the only one here with the good sense not to try to stand on skinny steel blades.

"Is this your first time on skates?" Blossom repeats.

"I told you I don't skate."

"I didn't think you meant you'd *never* skated. I thought all Canadians could skate."

"I guess you thought wrong."

"Slide back to the bench on your butt, then stand up using the bench."

Why did I think I could do this?

"Use your stick for balance," she tells me once I'm on my feet. My ankles ache, and my knees wobble. I feel like an old granny.

"First push with one skate, then the other," Blossom orders.

I try to move a skate to push, but the ice is too slippery. I slide my feet back together without moving forward. Blossom exhales loudly, takes my stick and stands it in the snow. Then she steps behind me and starts to push me gently around the rink.

The ice is bumpier than it looks. My skates chatter. The wind brushes my face. Except for the bumps, I feel like I'm flying.

"A little faster, Blossom," I whisper, and she pushes me faster. "Faster," I say, louder this time. Blossom pushes me faster. She gives me a solid push and lets go. I slide to a stop. "Watch," she says. "I'll show you how to move your feet so you can skate on your own."

SNAP! The ice cracks under my feet and shoots across the lake, thrumming like a too-tight guitar string. I jump at the sound and fall hard on my bum. More cracks echo back, deep and eerie, like the whale songs on one of Aunt Hannah's albums.

This is it; my life is over. Whales are waiting under the ice to swallow me. The ice will open up and close again before I can escape. I'll be trapped under enough ice to hold up an airplane.

8

"Blossom, help! The lake is splitting open!"

Murphy rushes over, panting dog breath in my face. Blossom laughs. "Wild, isn't it?" she says. Her laughter slices the frosty air like icicles. I have to remind myself to breathe.

"Wild? You call this wild? We could die out here." This whole place, inside and out, seems to want to crack apart from too much cold, too much snow, too much everything.

Murphy wags his tail and drools on me.

"The ice cracks like that all the time," Blossom says, offering me a hand up, "but it hasn't split open and swallowed anyone yet."

"H-how do you know it won't?"

Blossom shrugs. "You'll just have to trust me," she says. With great effort she pulls me to my feet and hands me a shovel. "Come on, we'll finish shoveling the rink while you get used to your skates. The shovel will help you with your balance. By the time we're done, you'll be ready to play some shinny, and we'll have the whole rink to skate on, not just this little bit."

Blossom starts to work. The way she hunkers down she looks more like she's trying to move a mountain than a fluffy layer of snow.

Does she think her one little skating demo has magically turned me into an NHL player? A Zamboni? She doesn't even look my way as she glides back and forth across the rink, pushing the shovel in front of her. I do my bum slide over to the bench and unlace my skates. Blossom ignores me. I pull on my cold boots. I could leave and

Blossom wouldn't even notice, but where would I go?

The ice is quiet now. For lack of anything better to do, I start clearing the end of the rink farthest away from her. We shovel in silence. Is this what happens when people move to the bush? Once they start talking, they can't stop; then when they finally stop, they forget how to start again.

"Must be almost lunchtime," Blossom says at last. "I guess the good old hockey game will have to wait."

"Works for me." No more shoveling, no skating and we get to eat.

Lunch is another huge meal. At least people eat well out here. When we're finished, Becky asks, "How about some snow ice cream for dessert?"

"Sure," Blossom replies.

"Snow ice cream?" My teeth shiver at the thought. Becky hands us each a big bowl. We bundle up again and head outside.

"Let Murphy in when you go out," Becky warns, "or we'll have dog hair in our ice cream." As soon as we're outside, Blossom calls Murphy and opens the door for him to run inside. Good thing. I don't think *dog hair* will make it as anyone's flavor of the month.

"No yellow snow in the bowl," Blossom warns. She must be thinking about Murphy too.

"Maybe we could make a snowman." I figure when life gives you snow, make a snowman. I scoop up a heap of snow and pat it between my mitts, but the harder I pat, the faster the snow falls apart. I pick up more snow, patting harder this time, but I get the same results.

"This snow makes good ice cream because it's so fluffy," Blossom tells me, "but it's too cold to stick together for snowballs or snowmen."

"Isn't all snow cold? What good is snow if you can't make anything out of it? There must be something we can make." I gather armfuls of snow and dump them in a pile. I try every way I can think of to stick the snow together, but nothing works. "Maybe we could try snow angels, Blossom," I say.

I look around me, but Blossom is gone. "Blossom?" I shout. "Blossom?"

From deep in the trees, she calls back to me. I follow the sound, but I don't see her anywhere. Visions of Sasquatches crash through my head. Still, I keep wading through the deep snow toward her voice. When I no longer hear her, I stop to listen. The world around me is silent and still.

Suddenly a big snowstorm dumps on my head. Before I can open my eyes, another blast hits me. I wipe snow off my face with my mitts.

"Heads up," Blossom's voice says, and I look up just in time to see her shake a snow-covered branch and drop another blizzard of snow on me. Perched on a heavy branch, she laughs hysterically. "For someone as afraid of everything as you are, you sure don't pay much attention," Blossom scolds.

"I was trying to follow your voice."

"Good plan, but the way you kept your eyes glued to your feet, I thought you were afraid your boots might take off without you."

"Very funny, Blossom. I suppose you'd do something different?"

"What if I'd been a hungry cougar, waiting to pounce on you for my supper?" she says as she climbs down the tree. "You need to look up once in a while and notice what's around you. That's all."

As soon as her feet hit the ground, I charge, flipping snow at her with both hands.

"Look, a snowman!" I shout. "A living, breathing snowman."

I splash snow at her for all I'm worth. She splashes me back. We storm through the trees, spinning like the snow devils on the lake. Snow drips down my neck in an icy trickle and fills my boots, but I won't stop. I go after her, arms flailing.

"Slow down," Blossom shouts. "Stop!" She turns to face me. "Stop!"

I flail faster, kicking snow too, with my boots.

Blossom trips and flops down flat on her back. I scoop snow over her, burying her in her own snowdrift.

She jumps up, pushes me down backward and scrubs my face with snow. It stings. I want to push her back, but she has her knee in my chest.

"Where's that snow for our ice cream?" Becky's voice calls faintly from the yard.

Blossom stops smearing snow on my face. "Coming," she calls sweetly.

"What's taking so long?" Becky calls again. "We're waiting."

Blossom moves her knee, and I stand up. Eyeing each other like two dogs, we fill our bowls with snow. I follow Blossom back to the house, surprised at how close it is. The forest felt far away.

"What took so long?" Aunt Hannah asks, looking squarely at me.

"Finding the perfect snow takes time," Blossom tells her.

Becky hands us each a wooden spoon and starts pouring canned milk mixed with sugar and vanilla over the snow in our bowls. "Keep stirring," she says, "if you want it creamy."

"Life in the bush must suit you, Emily,"

Aunt Hannah observes. "Look how rosy your cheeks are."

Blossom glares at me. I stir till my arm aches, then I switch hands and stir some more. Finally the snow starts to look creamy, almost like real ice cream.

"Not bad," I say, surprised by the smooth, rich taste. "Can I have more?"

"We have to eat it all," Becky says. "Snow ice cream doesn't keep."

I hold out my bowl.

9

As we're finishing our ice cream, Becky starts lighting oil lamps. I watch her strike a wooden match and lift a tall glass chimney. As she touches the match to the wick, a dark golden flame with a blue center leaps up. She replaces the chimney and turns down the wick, twisting what looks like a key on the side of the lamp. The deep gold turns a honey color and the room fills with soft light. The afternoon is slipping away. I look at my watch. It's only 2:30, but already the sun has dipped below the mountains.

"Before dark," Becky says, "I need you girls to bring in more firewood. We have a lot of cooking and baking to do tonight and tomorrow."

"More firewood?" I say. "I loaded that box up this morning."

"If we don't bring in more wood now, the box will be empty before morning. We use wood both for heating and cooking," Becky says as she sends us outside. "It's a little more work, but there are no monthly bills."

No monthly bills, eh? Maybe I should send her one. Hauling firewood, shoveling snow, hauling more wood. This is more like a torture test than a holiday.

At the woodshed, Blossom and I set up a system. She takes a piece of wood off the stack and hands it to me. I take the log, bend down and place it on the toboggan. Then I stand up and wait for her to hand me the next piece. This works fine until I have to fiddle with a log to fit it in place. Instead of standing up and waiting for Blossom to hand me the next one, I stand up just in time for her to clock me on the side of the head.

"Owww!"

"Are you okay?"

"I was until you clobbered me."

"Pay attention!"

"You're the one who wasn't paying attention."

"You can't even help with a simple chore like firewood."

"Fine. Firewood is my fault. Ice cracks are my fault. Snow, winter, you name it, and it's all my fault."

"Get a grip, Emily. We're getting firewood here, not running the universe."

Words fail me. I turn and run down the driveway. Purple and blue shadows swallow the snow. Soon it will be dark, but I don't care. I just want out of here.

"Emily," Blossom calls. "Emily!"

I keep running. Faster. Farther.

10

Blossom's driveway is long. Not at all like mine at home. Her driveway is just a wide path through the trees with snowbanks piled high on both sides. Nothing looks familiar. How could it? I was asleep when we drove in.

The path goes straight for a while, then makes a sharp turn to the right. I make the turn at full speed, as fast as I can in these big clunky boots. I don't look back, but I can still hear Blossom calling.

I clump down the road. Maybe that right turn put me on the road out of here, back to civilization. But no, in the distance I see a wider road. Which way to turn? I haven't a clue. Blossom is gaining on me. I run faster.

What if I don't make it anywhere before dark? That thought is too scary and cold to think about. What if I do get somewhere? What will I say when I get there?

I try to look around without slowing down. Up ahead I see hydro poles. There must be normal houses here somewhere with electricity and telephones. If someone will let me inside, I can call Mom and Dad and ask them to come get me. Would they? Would I wait at the stranger's house? Where else could I wait? Not at Blossom's.

"Emily!" Blossom calls.

I pull my neck down into my collar and run faster. I won't let Blossom catch me. I'll have to hide. But where?

I dive over the snowbank and roll into the soft snow behind it. I can hear Blossom coming closer. Snow clings to my clothes. It slips down my collar, so cold it burns my skin.

What to do? I stand up and try to run toward the road, but the snow is almost up to my armpits. It's like trying to run through water, only harder. In front of me is a wall of tangled branches and limbs. Even in summer I couldn't get through there. I curl up in the snow and wait for Blossom to pass.

Maybe she'll give up and go back home. After she's gone, I'll run down the road till I find a phone or a house. I hope it doesn't get too dark first. I hope no stray wolves find me. Or cougars.

A black shadow rises up over the snowbank. "Aaah!" I dive under the snow and scream until I choke.

"Easy, Emily," Blossom says. "It's only me."

"H-how did you find me?"

"Climb out of there and I'll show you."

For a moment I sit in the snow, choking, cold creeping into my bones. I want to be warm. And dry. I want to go home, but first I follow Blossom back over the snowbank.

"Look," Blossom says, showing me the line of boot prints going straight down the driveway, veering to the right and over the snowbank. "Just like connecting the dots." She smiles a big, freckly smile, looks me straight in the eye and says, "You're such a baby."

"I am not," I say.

"You are the King Kong of babies."

"And you're the biggest, fattest know-it-all I've ever met."

"I don't know it all, but I do know babies, and you're an even bigger baby than I was when we first moved here."

"What?" I say.

"Having you here was supposed to be fun for me, but when it comes to fun, you're clueless."

"How would you know what I am? You never shut up long enough to find out anything about me."

"Well, one thing I can tell you is you can't run away just because things don't go your way." Blossom starts walking back down the darkening road. "Believe me, I know. I've tried."

"What?" I say again, following her in spite of myself. "You ran away?"

"I've taken off at least once from just about everywhere we've lived. My latest attempt was from here, last summer. It was a lot warmer then than it is now. Buggier, too."

"Where did you go?"

"That's just it. It's too far to go anywhere."

I catch up to Blossom and walk beside her.

"We could run away together," I say. Annoying as she is, running away with her would be less scary than running away alone.

"I don't want to run away anymore. I like it here. It's beautiful. Look around you!"

"All I see are shadows, trees and snow," I tell her, leaving out the golden glow on the mountains and the deep shades of purple, orange and pink in the sky.

11

As we turn the corner toward Blossom's yard, I hear Aunt Hannah.

"Blossom! Emily! Where were you?" she yells, standing by our abandoned pile of firewood. "I came outside and couldn't find you anywhere."

"Sorry, Aunt Hannah," I say as we approach. My voice shakes. "I, um, had to use the outhouse and, uh, I guess I got turned around." What would she do if she knew I tried to leave?

"And I suppose you went to look for her, Blossom?"

"I found her, too," Blossom answers. I guess she doesn't like getting in trouble either.

"Didn't you hear me calling?"

"No."

"I was about to search the country for you."

"Sorry," Blossom mumbles.

"Honestly," Aunt Hannah says, turning back toward the house. "Is one simple chore too much to ask?"

Blossom watches her go with a long, low "Sheesh."

I shake my head.

"We have our orders," Blossom says.

"I guess so," I say. "But this time *I'll* take down the wood, and *you* stack it, okay?"

"Fine with me."

By the time we've hauled the last load of wood, it's dark. Inside the house, Aunt Hannah and Becky are zipping around like popped balloons.

"Emily, Blossom, how about peeling some apples for our pies," Aunt Hannah says, putting down her rolling pin. "Here you go."

"This is a whole box of apples," I say, staring.

Aunt Hannah hands Blossom and me each a peeler, a big bowl and a plastic bucket. "The bucket is for the peels and the bowl is for the apples. You'll be done in no time," she says.

Blossom and I raise our peelers and look at each other.

"I'll race you," Blossom says.

"Race me?"

"Whoever peels the fewest apples wins."

"Deal," I say, and we start peeling as slowly as we can.

Aunt Hannah and Becky keep dashing past, too busy to notice us, until on one of her passes, Aunt Hannah stops and frowns at our bowl. "I was hoping to have these pies before the next harvest, girls. Do you think you could work just a bit faster?"

Dale comes inside with a blast of icy air.

"Time to wash up for supper, girls," Becky announces as she sloshes a pot of cold water onto the stove. In the same breath she gives Aunt Hannah a hug and says,

"I don't know how we could have gotten ready for this party without you, Hannah!" Blossom and I throw our peelers into the bowl of apples.

During dinner, talk returns to the party.

"We told everyone to bring their favorite winter sports gear," Becky says, "so whether you want to ski, skate, snowshoe, toboggan or just sit by the fire, someone will be happy to join you."

"A few of us hardy ice fishermen will be setting up a hut on the lake, if you feel like fishing," Dale says, grinning so hard his teeth nearly swallow his beard.

"Fishing on ice? Brrr!" Just the thought of it turns my bones cold.

"Not for the faint of heart, I admit, but a whale of a good time. You'll have to try it, Emily. Then maybe Blossom will check it out too."

"Don't hold your breath on that one, Pop," Blossom says.

As the talk continues, I gather that a crowd of people will be showing up tomorrow and that we'll be plenty busy till they come. Dale won't go to the neighbor's tomorrow. He'll be shoveling parking areas and doing dozens of other things.

Maybe I can hitch a ride home with one of the guests. Surely someone will have room for me. One small person traveling light. Aunt Hannah can bring anything I leave behind.

Just as I'm finishing my third helping of mashed potatoes and gravy, Becky says, "Blossom and Emily, if you girls will do the dishes, the rest of us can get back to work."

"This never ends, does it?" I mutter to Blossom. "No wonder you don't have a television. You'd never have time to watch it."

"Yep, it's just a chore a minute around here," Blossom says. "And I almost forgot to tell you that we do have a farm animal here, one that needs constant feeding. Here you go, Porky." She scrapes a dish into the compost bucket.

Blossom turns her back to me, and I hear a loud "Chomp, chomp, slurp, smack."

When she faces me again, she says, "Go on, feed him. He's hungry."

I stare at her.

"Don't worry," she says. "Porky rarely bites. Right, Porko?"

"Slurp. Smack!" is the loud reply.

"Oooh-kay," I say, scraping a dish into the bucket.

After more loud chomping, Blossom shakes her head and says, "Ooh, Porky, you are such a noisy eater."

Once all the table scraps have been fed to Porky, Blossom and I start washing. Careful not to repeat our firewood accident, I slosh the dishes around in one basin, rinse them in anotherand hand them to Blossom, who dries them and puts them away. Becky and Aunt Hannah rush around behind us, taking out everything from flour and sugar to jars of tomatoes and peaches, along with pots, pans and baking dishes of every size and description. Dale starts preparing his special lasagna.

"Blossom, when you've finished the dishes, please beat these eggs," Becky says, taking out a large mixing bowl and an egg-beater. She sets these on the counter by a stack of egg cartons. "Six at a time."

I'm glad I don't have to do that. My arm is still tired from beating the snow ice cream and peeling apples. Maybe when she's finished I can lick the cake batter from the bowl. Or better yet, lick the icing bowl.

Becky hands me a grater and a big bag of carrots. "We need grated carrots for cake and salad," she tells me. I scowl. "Don't worry about washing or peeling them, dear. They're already washed. And besides," she pauses, smiling at Aunt Hannah, "they're organic. Straight from our very own garden."

Shadows flit around the kitchen in the lamplight. Becky starts singing, "Doo-wah diddy, diddy-dum, diddy-do." Dale and Aunt Hannah join in.

I grate carrots into a bowl while they sing every corny song that's ever been written. Dale assembles his lasagna and sits down at the piano.

The house fills with music. The fire pops and crackles like an offbeat drummer.

Flames flicker through the glass door of the big wood heater. Orange, red, yellow and black twist together and jump apart in a dance that's quiet and wild at the same time. My foot taps.

"That's a Scott Joplin tune I just learned," Dale tells us, and before anyone can say anything, he starts another one.

Still grating, I breathe in and fill my nose with smells of spicy tomato sauce, simmering chocolate, fried onions and freshly baked bread.

Ouch! I hope our guests will appreciate the extra protein they'll be getting from my knuckles. Blood is pretty nutritious too, if I remember right. Being the brave soul I am, I suck the blood from my knuckle and go back to grating. "Ouch!" More skin in the carrots. "OUCH!" I say again, more loudly. No one hears me. I drop the grater and suck my knuckles. No one notices. I head for the sink to rinse off the blood. On my way there I almost bump into Becky, who's carrying a big pot of pasta.

"Careful, Emily," Becky warns. "This water's boiling hot."

"Emily, pay attention," Aunt Hannah yells across the room. "Someone could get hurt."

"I'm already hurt," I shout, holding up my bloody knuckles. "Look!"

The music stops. "You'll be fine, just wash your hand in the sink when Becky is finished. We'll find you a couple of Band-Aids," Aunt Hannah says. "And be sure to fish any skin out of the carrots and rinse them."

"You care more about those stupid carrots than you do about me."

"Now, Emily..."

"Now Emily nothing," I shout, shaking my bleeding hand.

Aunt Hannah gives me a look that cuts deeper than the grater. "You scraped yourself, Emily, and we'll patch you up. It's no big deal."

I turn and run upstairs.

No one says anything. No one follows me. If Blossom's room had a door, I'd slam it.

12

The brittle silence is shattered by Aunt Hannah's voice. "Keep working, everyone. Don't worry about Emily. She just needs some attention. I'll go up and speak to her."

Can't Aunt Hannah keep her big mouth shut?

Slippered feet slap up the stairs. Half of me wants to hide under Blossom's bed. Half wants to grab Aunt Hannah and tear out handfuls of her frizzy hair. She walks into the room and locks her eyes on mine even though I want to look away.

"Emily, what was all that fuss about downstairs?"

"I cut myself. Remember?"

"You're upset about more than that. What's bugging you? Tell me."

"Nothing. Nothing. Just leave me alone." I want to run, but I don't know where to go. My eyes blur, and my lips won't stop trembling.

"I know this isn't the holiday you thought you wanted," Aunt Hannah says, sitting both of us down on Blossom's bed, "but I still thought it would be perfect for us."

"But why?" I ask, as tears run down my cheeks. "Why here? Why me?"

"I thought coming here would be a new experience for both of us. An adventure we could share."

"Well, it isn't an adventure, and we aren't sharing it. You're so busy with your friends you hardly know I'm here except to boss me around."

"Emily, that isn't fair."

"Fair? What's fair? Not you, not any of it. Now go away and leave me alone." I slide off the bed and climb down into my sleeping bag before Aunt Hannah can say anything else.

"Emily! Emily, come out and talk to me. Emily?"

I don't answer. Aunt Hannah waits. I can hear her breathing, loud huffs and puffs, like the Big Bad Wolf. At last she says, "Fine. If that's how you want it, that's how it will be. Fine."

I don't move. I barely breathe. Aunt Hannah's feet slap back down the stairs. Let her go. I don't care. When the guests come for the party, I'll leave with somebody else, and if I'm lucky, I'll never have to speak to the Big H again.

I hear muffled voices and then more footsteps on the stairs. I crawl down to the bottom of my sleeping bag in case Aunt Hannah is coming back with some new way to torture me.

"You can come out now," Blossom says. "It's only me with my handy first-aid kit. Come on, hold out your hand." I sit up and do as she says, biting my lips while she patches up my knuckles like a real nurse.

When she's finished, she looks at me, and my eyes fill with tears. "We might as well get ready for bed," she says. Still afraid to talk, I focus all of my attention on my pajamas. Blossom does the same. Everyone here hates me; I'm sure of it. I haven't brushed my teeth or washed my face or even gone to the outhouse, but I'd rather suffer all night than go downstairs now.

More footsteps on the stairs. I dive deep into the stuffy warmth of my sleeping bag, curl up with my pillow and pretend to be asleep. Even with my pillow wrapped around my ears, I can hear the stiff goodnights. The light goes out, and even though I don't want to, I start to cry. I shove my face into the pillow so Blossom won't hear me.

"You know," comes a voice from above my head, "for your first time on skates, you weren't all that bad today."

Did I hear her right? "What?" I say from deep inside my sleeping bag.

"I said I thought there might be some hope for you as a hockey player," she says, a little louder, "with a lot of practice, of course."

"Me?" I ask, sliding my head slowly out of the sleeping bag, like a turtle peeking out of its shell. I take a deep breath and wipe my sleeve across my face. Blossom's room is dark, but I can see her head over the edge of the bed.

"You *could* learn."

"I can't believe you're talking about hockey," I tell her. "You're only saying that because you want someone to shoot pucks with you."

"You think I'm that hard up for friends?"

"That's not what I meant."

"What *did* you mean?"

"I mean I'm sorry I'm not the hockey-crazy Canuck you were hoping for. I'm sure you'll have plenty of hockey-playing friends coming tomorrow for the party."

"No, I won't."

"No? Why not?"

"I just won't. That's all," Blossom whispers so softly I can barely hear her.

I take a deep breath. "Please don't be mad," I say, swallowing all my pride. "This holiday isn't what I was hoping for, but it's not your fault."

For a moment the room is silent, then Blossom says, "I invited Tricia and Amber, my best friends from Red Deer, but neither of them could come."

"Why not?"

"Tricia's family already made plans to go to Disneyland."

I feel a deep pain in my stomach. "What about Amber?" I ask.

"Amber's parents said they had other plans too. But in her letter, Amber said her dad thinks only crazy people would drive up here in the middle of winter. He thinks we're crazy for moving here."

"Maybe you won't have to stay."

"Maybe I won't be able to stay."

I'm not sure if Blossom's about to cry or fall asleep. I try to imagine being her, stuck here. What would it be like? She says she never gets to stay anywhere for very long, so she probably won't be here long either.

"My friends and I always start out saying we'll be friends forever," Blossom says, "no matter what. But then I move away, and after a while they just seem to disappear."

"I've never moved anywhere, but my friends disappear too."

I can hear Blossom breathing, but she doesn't say anything. "Have you made any friends here yet?" I wait a long time for her to answer, but she doesn't.

Finally she says, "Don't let your aunt bug you, Emily. Before you came, my mom told me Hannah was totally stressed out and bossy, but she likes her anyway."

"She's a big bully," I say. My throat tightens.

"So, no one's perfect. The question is, are you going to let her bully you out of your holiday?"

For what seems like the hundredth time tonight, I don't know what to say. The wind outside presses against the windows. I squeeze my eyes shut and pull my sleeping bag over my head.

13

"Now this is what I call snow!" I hear Dale say before I even open my eyes in the morning. I open my eyes slowly, remembering yesterday's painful awakening, and look out Blossom's window. The air is thick with swirling snowflakes. I leap out of my sleeping bag, nearly ripping it apart as I trip on its tight opening, and stumble to the window.

All I see is white. White everywhere. What if there's no party? What if I'm snowed in here with Aunt Hannah till spring? I dress quickly and hurry downstairs.

"Lots of shoveling today, campers," Dale says as I join everyone in the kitchen.

"Every shovel we can lay our hands on will have to be pushed into action."

Becky smiles at me and hands me a plate piled high with pancakes. Blossom is too busy eating to look up. Maybe everyone has forgotten last night.

"How are those knuckles, Emily?" Dale asks. "Do you think you'll be able to handle a shovel?"

All eyes turn to me. I put my plate down and flex my fingers. "No problem, Dale," I say. "I'm ready for anything." I glance up at Aunt Hannah, who opens her mouth to say something, but before she can say a word, I quickly ask, "Are the roads snowed in?"

"Buried deep," Dale says cheerfully. "Probably will be for most of the day. We're not much of a priority out here."

I avoid Aunt Hannah's eyes. "Is the party canceled?" I ask. If it is, what will I do?

"The road should be cleared before our guests start to arrive," Becky says. "We just have to make sure they can get in and have a place to park."

"I hope you girls can keep that skating rink clear," Aunt Hannah says, though I'm sure that wasn't what she started to say before. "I can hardly wait to strap on my skates."

"You're a real Canadian, Aunt Hannah," I tell her.

"Before we came you called me un-Canadian. Now I'm a real Canadian. Which is it, Emily? Make up your mind." Aunt Hannah laughs.

With a look that could turn maple syrup to gasoline, I ignore her question. "Won't the rink just get covered up again if it keeps snowing?" I ask.

"We can only handle so much snow at a time," Dale explains. "If we have to shovel twice, we'll shovel twice. If I don't plow our driveway with the truck before the main road is cleared, we'll have an extra mountain of snow to move."

My bladder reminds me of my hurried departure to bed last night. I hope my pillow rubbed any tear streaks off my cheeks. I hand my breakfast plate back to

Becky. "Nature's calling," I tell her. "I'll be right back."

"I'll keep this warm for you," Becky says as I bundle up and head outside.

With all the snow, it's hard to tell where the path is. I look around, trying to get my bearings. Becky taps on the window and points me in the right direction.

Back in the house, I wash up and brush my teeth, avoiding eye contact with Aunt Hannah while I eat my pancakes.

No homework today. After breakfast, Blossom and I bundle up and head outside. I know the routine now. Firewood first. Blossom is careful not to hit me in the head. I keep a close eye on her anyway.

We fill the woodbox and are about to pack our shovels down to the skating rink when we see Aunt Hannah head for the outhouse.

"You were pretty mad at your aunt last night," Blossom says.

"I was hoping you'd forget about that."

"Forget it without getting even first?" Blossom asks, a strange new glint in her eyes.

Before I can ask what she means, she puts a finger to her lips to shush me. We rest our shovels on the trail to the rink and wait till Aunt Hannah closes the outhouse door.

"Are you thinking what I think you are?" I whisper.

"Yep," Blossom says, "but I'm going to let you do the honors. Run for it; you don't have much time."

As quickly and quietly as I can, I run up to the outhouse and latch the door. Blossom has my shovel waiting for me. She hands it to me, and I follow her to the rink, running all the way. Murphy lopes down the hill after us.

"I think I heard some serious banging on the outhouse door," Blossom says and bursts out laughing.

"I think I heard some yelling too," I add.

"We'd better start pushing snow," Blossom says. "We'll need an alibi."

The more I think of Aunt Hannah trapped in the outhouse, the harder I shovel. When we've cleared about half the rink, I say,

"Can't we just shovel this much today and finish it tomorrow when there are more people to help? Who's going to skate in the dark?"

"It's a full moon tonight," Blossom tells me. "The skating should be great, if it's clear."

"Moonlight skating," I say out loud, trying to picture it.

While we're shoveling, the snowflakes get bigger and start falling farther apart. I stick out my tongue, hoping to catch one.

The clouds thin out. The dull circle in the sky turns out to be the sun. Across the lake a shadowy shape stretches slowly toward us.

"Look," I whisper, poking Blossom's arm and pointing, "a deer! It's huge!"

"I don't think it's a deer," Blossom whispers back.

"What is it then? A cow? A horse? I didn't think horses got that big."

Blossom squints down the lake. "Shh," she whispers. "I think it's a moose."

The shape moves closer. Murphy hides behind us. Sunshine sparkles on the snow as the moose's shadow darkens and stretches. The huge animal wades effortlessly through chest-deep snow. I remember myself yesterday, struggling through much less snow than that.

I stand with Blossom and Murphy, listening to my heart beat, beat, beat. The moose wanders through a tangle of red and yellow bushes into a clump of trees and disappears.

"Amazing," I whisper to Blossom.

"You won't find any real moose in Disney..." Blossom begins, but her voice is drowned out by a high-pitched wail, moving closer and getting louder. Murphy starts to bark.

The noise gets louder. A deep rumble, rising to a roar. A helicopter? An airplane? I look up at an empty sky, then back at Blossom. I follow her eyes with mine.

A low-riding machine crests a hill onto the lake. Could all that howling be coming from one small machine? A Harley roaring down our street purrs like a kitten in comparison.

The machine heads straight for us.

At the last second it turns and spins a powdery snow donut. Murphy crouches down and growls. The machine keeps spinning. Finally it slows down. Could the heat from all that spinning melt the ice and send us to the bottom of the lake?

Two thick-mittened hands adjust a visor on a silver helmet. Murphy hides behind Blossom. My mouth hangs open. One mittened hand waves briefly while the other revs up the engine. A muffled voice shouts something like "Sea duh ton ite." A moment later the machine speeds off and disappears over the horizon, leaving Blossom, Murphy and me standing like snow sculptures.

"What was that?" I ask when the noise finally dies down.

"Billy Olson with his new snowmobile," she says.

"What?" I ask again.

"Billy Olson lives on the ranch down the road. His family has been here for something like a hundred years. He's the only

117

person around who's anywhere close to my age."

"Are you friends?" I ask. "Will he come back and take us for a ride?"

"I wouldn't count on it," Blossom says, scrunching her freckles.

"Why not?" I ask. We finally see another kid who is actually doing something interesting, and Blossom doesn't seem to care. Why?

Blossom doesn't answer. I wait. She starts shoveling again. I ask an easier question. "Do you have a snowmobile? They look like fun."

"The only snow machine we have, besides Blizzard Buster and me, of course, is our trusty toboggan," she replies.

Why am I not surprised?

14

By the time we get back to the house, three vehicles are parked in the yard. Becky is directing someone toward the outhouse.

"Leave the door ajar," she says. "I had to rescue Hannah earlier today because the outside latch slipped shut while she was inside. That only happened once before, to the little neighbor boy down the road, but I won't let it happen again. As soon as you're finished, I'll pull the latch off so no one else will have any trouble."

Blossom and I hurry inside, hoping no one sees us laughing.

People keep driving in by the truckload, with boxes full of food. Many have sleeping gear. The upstairs floor has wall-to-wall sleeping bags. Fortunately Blossom's room is too small for anyone else to move in.

Avoiding Aunt Hannah isn't hard; a chatter of people surrounds her. She gives me an "I want to talk to you" look, but I smile and nod, keeping my distance. By dinnertime, the house is filled with people.

"Do you know all these people?" I ask Blossom.

"Most of them," she replies, "some more than others."

"Who are they?" If I really want to go home with someone besides Aunt Hannah, I'll need to find out who's going back to Vancouver so I can set up my ride.

"That's my Aunt Sami over there with Uncle Robert. And that's my baby cousin, Sadye."

"Where do they live?" I ask.

"Edmonton."

Forget Edmonton. "Who's the lady with the red scarf around her neck?"

"She's my mom's best friend, Jane."

"Where does she live?"

"Chilliwack."

Closer. "Did she come up alone?" Will Blossom guess why I'm asking?

"Why do you want to know?" she asks, looking me straight in the eye.

"Just curious. She must be brave to drive here alone. Did she?"

"Yes," Blossom answers. "She's very brave."

To draw attention away from people old enough to drive, I ask, "Who's that squirt running around and sliding on his socks?"

"That's Billy Olson."

"Billy Olson? But he's just a little kid! He can't be much older than my brother."

"Tell me about it," Blossom says with a sigh.

"He looked much bigger on the snowmobile."

"That's what a helmet will do for you."

Billy runs up to us making sputtering engine noises, spitting all over us.

"Buzz off, Billy!" Blossom shouts.

And Billy does, still buzzing around the room. No wonder Blossom wasn't talking about him. How do you make friends with a spluttering engine?

"There *are* people here from Vancouver who would probably be happy to take you home, if you asked them."

"What? Who told you I wanted to go home?"

"As my dad would say, it isn't exactly rocket science. Why else would you ask where everyone lived?"

I stare at Blossom, not knowing what to say. "Do you want me to leave?" I ask.

"If that's what you want to do, but no one's leaving yet. You might as well eat first."

People are uncovering salads and pulling dishes from the oven. A big buffet table made of sawhorses and plywood covered with a flowered sheet sags under the weight of stews, soufflés, roast meat, fresh bread, vegetables and at least ten different kinds of salad. The desserts are crowded in the kitchen, waiting for their turn on the table.

Aunt Hannah places little paper name-tags beside each dish. Rabbit stew with noodles, short ribs of venison, wild rice with shaggy manes. What is this stuff? Do people really eat it?

Blossom and I each take a plate. She piles hers high. I guess all that practice stacking firewood might be good for something after all. I read the nametag beside each dish, sticking with chicken, mashed potatoes, buttered buns and Jell-O with pears, careful to avoid the carrot salad.

Sitting on a chair with my food in my lap, I watch Aunt Hannah pick her way around the table: mashed turnips, bread with no butter, a sampler of salads. No carrot salad for her either.

Desserts are more familiar: apple pie, chocolate cake, pumpkin squares, Nanaimo bars. I have room for all of them on my plate and in my belly, except for carrot cake, of course.

After dinner and dessert, the dishes are cleared away, then the table. The only furniture left in the room is Dale's piano and some chairs. Two people take out guitars. Aunt Hannah tunes her fiddle. Someone strums a banjo and the music begins. Toes tap and people start to dance.

Checking out rides will be harder than I thought. Unlike the grown-up parties at home, people seem to have come here for music and dancing—not talk. If I'm going to find a ride, I'll have to shout over the music.

First things first, though. I have to go to the outhouse. I don't want to go alone, but Blossom is on the other side of the room, holding her new baby cousin. I can't wait for her.

"Hey, guess what?" Billy Olson has plowed through the crowd to stand nose to nose with me.

"What?" I say, my voice short and impatient.

"My dad says we can come over tomorrow and take people for rides on our snowmobiles. Wanna go?"

"Sure," I say. "I might be going home tomorrow, but if I'm still here, I'll be the first one in line."

"Great," he says. "Wanna dance?"

"I have to go outside," I tell him.

"Okay, let's go."

"To the outhouse," I blurt out.

"Oh," Billy says. "Well, see you later." He scoots off and leaves me standing alone. Alone to go outside into the frozen night.

Once more I bundle up in boots, scarf, jacket and mitts. I take the flashlight that's been left by the door. When I open the door, a steamy cloud pushes its way inside, billowing up like one of the clouds over the hot dinner dishes. Instead of spicy warmth, though, all I smell is cold. I step outside and close the door. Music follows me down the path.

"I thought the outhouse was closer than this," I mutter. I keep my head down, careful to stay on the path. I thought I knew exactly where to go. And I really *have* to *go*. Now!

I look behind me. The house is still there. I can still hear music. The outhouse can't be far. I walk faster. But instead of the outhouse, I've found the toolshed. No time to be picky. I walk around the side of the shed and kick a hole in the snow. After fumbling through my layers of clothes, I drop my pants with great relief.

Once I'm back together again, I look for the house. I walk around the corner of the shed. There's a trail. This must be the way I came. I can still hear the music. I start following the sound, but I don't see the house. Am I on the right path? I walk faster, but my foot slips, and I slide into the snow.

I try to stand up, but the snow is deep. I slip again. Pushing with all my might, I lift up. But I've pushed too hard, and I tumble down the hill.

When I finally roll to a stop, I stand up carefully. With my free hand, I brush the snow off my clothes and the flashlight. At least it still works. What do I do now?

I can still hear music, but I can't tell where it's coming from. I see a pale light in the distance. It doesn't seem to be where I remember the house, but I walk toward it anyway. What other light could there be?

Walking through the deep snow is slow and cold. Why didn't I pay more attention when I was walking with Blossom? I look ahead and see an open area. The lake! If I can make it to the skating rink, maybe I'll be able to find my way back to the house.

15

I take one step, stop cold and scream for all I'm worth. Something is following me! I try to run, but the snow fights every step. What is it? A madman? A cougar? A wolf?

I fall down, get up and start running again. Still running, I try to look behind me. I run faster. I listen, but I can't hear anything. I run and run. Then I look beside me, and there it is!

My shadow. The terrible monster that was following me was my shadow.

Good thing no one saw me. I take some deep breaths and point myself toward the rink. While I catch my breath, I listen to the lake. It sounds like all kinds of fish beating their tails against the ice, thrumming it like a drum. Big fish, giant fish, whales maybe.

But if I can make it to the rink, I should be able to find the trail back to the house. I step as lightly as I can. If the ice opens now and swallows me, no one will know where I am, and I won't float to the surface until spring. A shiver runs down my spine, but I keep walking.

When I reach the bench, I sit down. What now? A maze of paths crisscrosses the lake. Which one leads back to Blossom's? Billy's snowmobile tracks wind through the tracks Blossom and I made earlier. What if I follow the wrong tracks and get really lost?

The lake is still thunking, and I can still hear a murmur of music, but I can't tell where it's coming from. I close my eyes and lie down on the bench to think.

Will I freeze to death? Will wild animals eat me? A tear rolls down my cheek into my ear. I open my eyes and nearly fall off the bench.

Stars! Millions, billions, zillions of stars spill across the sky. More stars than I ever imagined burn fiery bright over the mountains. Every crystal of snow sparks with starlight.

I have to remind myself to breathe.

Only my breath, floating in a cloud above my face, lies between me and the stars. Soft chords of music from the house drift through the air. The lake thrums the bass.

With my eyes fixed on the sky, I stand up, stretch out my arms and sway to the music. Back and forth. Back and forth. Like a tree in the wind. Slowly at first. Then faster.

I slide one foot forward on the ice, then the other. Left, push, glide. Right, push, glide. My feet are light as leaves. The wind on my face is cool and alive.

My shadow glides along beside me, soft as the starlight. Lift, glide, spin, fly. I'm floating over a sea of snow.

Dancing with the stars.

The world grows lighter and lighter until an enormous light rises over the moun-

tains. The full moon! My shadow leaps across the snow.

"EMILY!"

I look across the rink. A line of bobbing toques and flashlights is coming from the party.

Aunt Hannah leads the parade.

"Emily! Emily!" Aunt Hannah calls, running toward me. "I've been trying to catch up with you all day."

I fill my lungs with cold, sharp air.

When she reaches me, Aunt Hannah stops to catch her breath. I watch mine escape in a big white cloud.

"Emily," she says at last, "you were right."

"What?"

"You were right. I haven't been fair. I've been so wrapped up with my own friends and my own holiday that I haven't taken time to think about you or your holiday."

I stare at my aunt.

"When I was stuck in the outhouse earlier today..."

Uh-oh.

"...I began to realize what you were trying to tell me. You feel as trapped here as I did in that outhouse."

"About that, Aunt..." I begin.

"Can we just start fresh, dear?"

"Sure, Aunt Hannah. Fresh is good. It's great."

For the first time I can remember, Aunt Hannah has nothing to say. She just smiles a big, goofy smile.

"I'm going to go get Blossom now," I tell her. "She's teaching me how to skate."

Aunt Hannah is still smiling as I run over to the bench, pick up my flashlight, flick it off and slip it in my pocket. Finding my way back to the house will be easy.

The string of guests will guide me.

Acknowledgments

Emily's story has grown slowly over the years. I would like to thank everyone who helped her find her way into this book, including those at our local newspaper who first started me thinking about a winter story; Dennis Johnson and Doris Laner, who showed interest in the story as a picture book, and Ann Featherstone, who suggested telling even more about Emily. At Sage Hill in Saskatchewan, our instructor, Kit Pearson, and my fellow writers (Martha, Jo, Cathy, Sheena and Norma) offered the guidance I needed to develop my first draft. Later, Norma, Ann, Linda, Ellen, Joan and Becky offered solid assistance when I thought I'd lost my way. I also owe special thanks to Orca Book Publishers, my wonderful editor, Maggie deVries, and the B.C. Arts Council, for their support and encouragement.

Kathleen Cook Waldron lived for thirteen years in a log home that she and her husband built. They had no electricity, no running water, no road for the first five years, and she homeschooled their two children until there were ten children in the area, enough to open a one-room school. Visitors would ask Kathleen, "What do you do all day out here?" In *Five Stars for Emily*, Emily learns what Kathleen learned long ago: that there is more to the simple things of life than someone used to malls and movies might at first realize.

Orca Young Readers
*New titles this season in **bold***

Daughter of Light	martha attema
Hero	martha attema
Things Are Looking Up, Jack	Dan Bar-el
Dog Days	Becky Citra
Flight from Big Tangle	Anita Daher
Chance and the Butterfly	Maggie deVries
Dinosaurs on the Beach	Marilyn Helmer
Birdie for Now	Jean Little
Catching Spring	Sylvia Olsen
The Reunion	Jacqueline Pearce
Jesse's Star	Ellen Schwartz
The Keeper and the Crows	Andrea Spalding
Phoebe and the Gypsy	Andrea Spalding
Jo's Triumph	Nikki Tate
Just Call Me Joe	Frieda Wishinsky

Max and Ellie series by Becky Citra:
Ellie's New Home, The Freezing Moon,
Danger at The Landings, Runaway

TJ series by Hazel Hutchins:
TJ and the Cats, TJ and the Haunted House,
TJ and the Rockets

Basketball series by Eric Walters:
Three on Three, Full Court Press, Hoop Crazy!
Long Shot, Road Trip, Off Season
Underdog